Cai Lun

The Creator of Paper

Story and Illustrations: Li Jian
Translation: Yijin Wert

Editors: Wu Yuezhou, Anna Nguyen
Editorial Director: Zhang Yicong

ISBN: 978-1-60220-996-1

Address any comments about *Cai Lun—The Creator of Paper* to:

Shanghai Press and Publishing Development Co., Ltd.
Floor 5, No. 390 Fuzhou Road, Shanghai, China (200001)
Email: sppd@sppdbook.com

Printed in China by Shanghai Donnelley Printing Co., Ltd.

3   5   7   9   10   8   6   4   2

蔡伦
Cai Lun

The Creator of Paper

by Li Jian

Translated by Yijin Wert

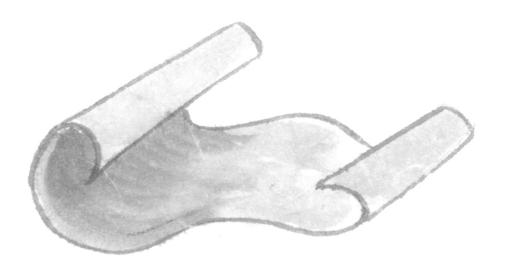

Better Link Press

Cai Lun was born in a farmer's family.
At the age of 15, he was called into the
Palace to serve the Emperor.

蔡伦出生于农家，十五岁的时候，
被选进宫里做侍从。

Cai Lun was very smart and good at studying, which soon led to his promotion as an official in charge of documentation and delivering messages.

蔡伦聪明伶俐，善于学习，不久被提拔为皇帝的侍从官，负责掌管文书、传达命令。

Cai Lun felt the job was hard work. At that time, documents were either written on a tablet of bamboo strips or on silk. One tablet of bamboo strips could only hold a few words. The memorial to the throne or official communication to the Emperor was usually very heavy, not to mention a book which required several people to transport.

蔡伦觉得管理这些文书异常辛苦。因为当时的文字都写在竹简或缣帛上。一条竹简写不了几个字，奏章已经很重了，一部书更是需要几个人搬动。

The silk was light, but normally too expensive. Cai Lun often wondered if there was another material that would be suitable for writing.

缣帛虽然轻薄，但很昂贵。蔡伦常常想：有没有一种更适合记录文字的东西呢？

One day, Cai Lun saw some thin matted sheets that came from a silk maker. He thought these sheets could be suitable material for writing on.

有一天，蔡伦看到了一个丝绸生产商进贡的一些丝质薄片，他觉得这些薄片很适合书写文字。

Cai Lun visited the silk-making place. There he saw the maid unwinding the thread and leaving the cocoons on a mat to dry. This left a thin white layer of a slightly fluffy substance that could be used for writing. However, it would be difficult to produce a large quantity of these thin matted sheets.

蔡伦来到这些薄片的故乡，看见抽完丝的蚕茧被留在席子上，晒干后就成了薄薄的一片，这薄片可以被用来写字。但这样的薄片不能大量生产。

Feeling inspired Cai Lun began experimenting with various materials such as dry grass, tree bark and cloth ... He filled his home full of raw goods in a quest to find one that could be mass-produced for paper.

聪慧的蔡伦受到启发，开始试验，干草、树枝、棉布……他的住所一下成了杂物铺，只为找到一种可以用来大量制造纸张的材料。

Unfortunately, Cai Lun failed to make any progress after many attempts.

可是，蔡伦试验了很久也没有什么进展。

The Emperor showed great enthusiasm for Cai Lun's paper-making experiments. He sent Cai Lun over to the Department of Tool Making in the Palace for help.

皇帝对蔡伦造纸的实验很感兴趣，派蔡伦去皇宫里制造器物的机构寻求帮助。

In the department, Cai Lun became friends with many skilled craftsmen, who threw their support behind his project. This propelled him to finally succeed in improving paper making.

First, they chopped tree bark into small pieces and removed all of the foreign objects.

蔡伦在那儿认识了很多能工巧匠，得到了强大的技术支持，他的想法终于实现了。

首先，他们将树皮剪碎切断，并去除杂质。

Then they soaked the chopped bark in plant ash water to decompose any remain foreign objects. A fine fiber was left behind.

将切碎的树皮浸泡在草木灰水里，过了一段时间，其中的杂物腐烂了，而不易腐烂的纤维留了下来。

Next, the fiber was drained, steamed on a fire,
and then ground into a fiber pulp in a stone grinder.

工匠们捞起浸泡过的原料，生火将它们蒸
软，再放入石臼中，捶打成糊状。

After this, they stirred the fiber pulp into a massive trough.

再把这些糊状的纤维放进水槽里搅拌，打成浆状。

The workers scooped out the fiber pulp with a bamboo strainer. They squeezed out any remaining water before laying it on a wooden board to dry.

这时用竹篾把絮状纤维抄起来，压出水分，贴在木板上晒干。

Once dried and removed from the wooden board, it was a light paper with a soft texture that could be stored away.

揭下晒干的纸，就是又轻又薄、质地柔软、可以贮存的纸了。

Cai Lun succeeded in making paper that was light and thin, strong and inexpensive by using rags, broken fishing nets and hemp ropes.

蔡伦又用布头、破旧的渔网、麻绳等材料，成功地造出了既轻又薄、既结实又廉价的纸张。

The Emperor spoke highly of Cai Lun's creation, and ordered it to be officially used in the country.

With the invention of a cheap and easy production process, Cai Lun's paper-making technique was well received by the society.

皇帝对蔡伦造出的纸大加赞赏，并下令向全国推广。

蔡伦造纸原料低廉、工艺简单，很快就受到了人们的欢迎。

Cai Lun's invention was also introduced to other countries. This allowed them to document, share, develop, and pass down their culture from generation to generation with affordable paper.

蔡伦的造纸术也传播到了其他国家，各国的文化都因为有了这种低廉的纸，而得以记载、传播、发展和传承。

Today, paper is part of our everyday lives. It would be hard to imagine what we could do without it.

今天，纸已经融入我们生活的方方面面，很难想象没有纸我们的生活会变成什么样子。

Cultural Explanation
知识点

Before Cai Lun invented paper, writings in China were generally made on the various materials including:

蔡伦发明造纸术之前，中国人曾经使用过各种材料用于书写：

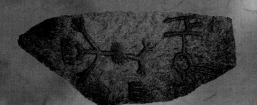

Stone
石头

Tortoiseshell
龟甲

Pottery
陶器

Bronze vessel
钟鼎

Bamboo scroll
竹简

Silk scroll
丝绸